ANDY ROBERTS – circus rigger

GIORGIO FABRINI – Circus rigger

CHARLIE CHEERFUL (Angus Campbell) - Clown

QUICKSILVER (Louisa Turner) Trapeze artist

IAN MADDOCK – Circus Rigger

WILLIAM NORTHROP – circus manager

PHILLIP HOSKINS – Safety Inspector

SOMETIMES CLOWNS EVEN CRY

"Ladies and Gentlemen, small children and big children, young or old ... welcome to The Circus Maximus."

Two performers dressed in the costumes of Roman gladiators stepped forward holding spears and trying to look fierce and intimidating as they stood either side of the ringmaster.

"*Who will fight me?*" one of them called out as he shifted his gaze along and over the tiers of wooden seating. A young lad of six or seven called out, "*I will!*" and some of the spectators laughed but then gasped as he rose from his bench and squeezed past them and along the bench to an aisle.

"This young fellow is a brave lad. He dares to approach whilst you remain in your seats. Ringmaster ... he has earned a laurel wreath in recognition of his bravery in coming forward. Ringmaster ..."

The ringmaster was handed a laurel wreath by one

of the high-wire performers. He took it from her and placed it on the boy's head.

"May the Gods protect you," he said as the audience applauded and stamped their feet.

The immediate razzmatazz over, a small band struck up a circus screamer, a frenzied melody full of fanfares and showy features that demonstrated and stretched their ability to play at around two hundred beats a minute.

Wandering around the outer circle of the ring was a white-faced figure with a bald head and a bright red and a bushy ring of hair that reached to his shoulders. He carried his usual bunch of coloured balloons in one hand and pretended to trip over his feet on which he wore a pair of giant-sized shoes.

The clown feigned fear as the band struck up *'Entrance of the Gladiators'* and two performers dressed as gladiators moved slowly towards him with swords raised. As they stepped closer, he backed away, put his hands to his mouth and began biting his nails. He began to wail and raised his arms towards the audience who laughed at his antics and pretended they were Caesar by making 'thumbs down' gestures to the gladiators. With a balloon in each hand, the clown began beating the warriors who, in turn, acted as if they were terrified of him and backed away. Soon after, the band struck up a raucous melody, the gladiators and the clown bowed theatrically and pushed through the backstage curtain and disappeared from view.

Backstage, behind the curtain and unseen by the audience, the mood was somewhat different.

"You need to watch that pretty little head of yours," Andy said as he brandished his gladiator's sword and poked its wooden tip into Georgio's stomach.

"Don't do that," Georgio snapped.

"I'll do as I please," Andy sneered. "You should join Charlie Cheerful in the ring. You're a bigger clown outside the ring than in it."

On the other side of the curtain the ringmaster's voice boomed out as he turned towards the three tightly-packed tiers of seating occupied by youngsters.

"Would one of you volunteer to climb the rope

ladder and stand on the platform?"

He raised his arm and pointed to a wooden platform.

"All you have to do is climb this ladder ..." and he pointed to a vertical set of metal steps that rose ten metres to a small wooden platform ... "and swing on the metal ring. I'll catch you if you fall."

"*You!*" he called out and beckoned to a lad aged about ten years. The boy stared open-mouthed at the structure and shook his head vigorously.

"What about *you*?" he asked, this time pointing to

a young girl who immediately burst into tears.

"No volunteers, then? Well, I guess we'll need to call back the gladiators."

"I'll do it!"

"Well, thank goodness Quicksilver is here! Are you feeling brave? Are you feeling courageous?"

Quicksilver raised an arm and walked slowly towards the metal steps that led to the platform.

"What do you think?" he asked the audience. "Should we let her risk her life on the trapeze?"

There were enthusiastic cries of '*yes*' from the youngsters. Their parents joined in their response although none showed any desire to climb the steps themselves.

The band played subdued music whilst the drummer punched loud single beats on his bass drum.

Quicksilver placed a foot on the lowest rung of the ladder, turned sideways and waved her right hand at her audience. She continued to climb, each step accompanied by a drumbeat until she reached the final rung at which point she looked down upon the forty-two feet wide circus ring, the same diameter, in fact, as the original ring at Philip Astley's circus amphitheatre.

Giorgio peered through a small gap in the curtains at the back of the ring and felt his heartbeat quicken. It was always the same. Every performance, every rehearsal, in fact, he felt the tension within his body increase. Quicksilver was an accomplished gymnast, a winner of numerous trophies and an international performer before joining a circus

Andy's sneered comments had stung. It was an open secret amongst the circus personnel that Giorgio was strongly attracted to Quicksilver who, beyond the circus, was better known as Louisa, a one-time teaching assistant in her hometown of Rochdale. Unbeknown to them, however, was that Andy Roberts, a member of the construction crew, harboured thoughts of a relationship with Alice and was resentful of the smiles and kisses blown from the palm of her hand in Giorgio's direction.

Quicksilver took the final step up from the ladder and now stood on the small platform above the ring. Glancing down before the circus light dimmed, she saw the blurred shapes of countless faces bathed in semi-darkness. This was always the moment her body would begin to tremble and she had to stiffen her legs to steady them. It was always the same. *She was terrified ...* not that she would ever admit it, not to herself or those around and beneath her in the audience. She was aware of the thoughts many of them harboured in the darker recesses of their minds. *What if she mistimed a move? What if her foot slipped on a bar or her hand failed to grasp a ring? Would there be a time when light-headedness left her faint or giddy and she slipped or passed out?*

Quicksilver shuddered when she recalled reading about Dessi Espana many years ago. Dessi was an aerial chiffon acrobat at Ringling Brothers and Barnum & Bailey circus in May 2004. She, too, had climbed up on to a wooden platform. Performing a difficult move, she had wrapped the chiffon around one leg and as she gracefully stretched out an arm, the hook holding the transparent fabric in place pulled lose and Dessi fell to the ground. She later died in hospital from her injuries and for a time the owners of the circus and newspapers looked into the possibility that it had been an intentional act on the part of a circus worker with a grievance. However, it was eventually determined to be an accident due to a technical failure.

*

A technical failure, Andy thought. *They'll put it down to a technical failure.* He had been one of three men in the small team that had secured the beam to which Quicksilver's rope was attached. If he couldn't hold her in his arms he'd make darned sure nobody else could either.

Quicksilver's heart missed a beat. The rope had too much play in it. It should be taut. She should be perfectly horizontal but her head had begun to angle down. The tensioner cable must have been set wrongly. Nobody would hear her if she called out and even if they did there was nothing rapid they could do. There was no safety net. Below her there was the sawdust ring which might keep the circus dry, clean, and sweet smelling ... and be good for soaking up blood.

* * *

Whenever his duties allowed, Giorgio found

pleasure in watching Quicksilver's aerial display. He thought she was beautiful, graceful and lithe. He hadn't the courage to tell her outright how he felt but it was common knowledge amongst those working in *The Circus Maximus* that he harboured romantic thoughts towards her.

He watched now as, high above him, she draped her limbs around a long band of white silk. A spotlight played on her figure and the spectators gasped as she stretched out first an arm, and then a leg ... and then she was no longer horizontal! The audience assumed that what they were observing was part of her routine.

But Giorgio knew different. Something was amiss with the rigging. He, Andy Roberts and Ian Maddock had been the team assigned to setting up the apparatus. They were experienced and not prone to error. They couldn't afford to be. Lives were at risk.

"*Somebody get the ladder!*" Giorgio yelled.

The ringmaster ran towards Giorgio and looked up. Quicksilver was now hanging on to the chiffon with both hands but the beam to which the silk was attached was being wrenched from its mounting. Two crew-members ran forward, one either side of a safety ladder that had been stored behind the curtain at the back of the ring. They were joined by Giorgio who began to ascend it, taking the rungs rapidly, climbing ever closer to Quicksilver. He reached out to her and at that moment she screamed.

The beam was shifting again, unable to remain secure, no longer locked in position

with the weight of Quicksilver dragging it down. If he didn't act instantly she would hurtle to the ground, a drop of ten metres. It would almost certainly be enough to kill her.

Giorgio reached out to her buy she failed to grab his hand. She still held the chiffon in her other hand, afraid to let go.

"I'll come closer. Try to get hold of me." he shouted. She screamed and dropped another metre. Giorgio braced himself on the ladder and extended his arm again. He gasped as his foot slipped and he was pitched down a rung.

Recovering his balance, he tried again.

"*Grab my hand,*" he yelled.

Quicksilver swung to and fro several times and was finally able to grab his hand. As she did so, the support beam snapped in two. One part crashed to the ground but the other remained dangling from its fixing point. She screamed.

"Reach up. Catch hold of the ladder!" he yelled. Quicksilver thought she might faint.

Two crew members shifted the safety ladder slightly and Quicksilver was able to grab a rung, pull it closer and hug the ladder. She was terrified and felt she might pass out at any moment.

"I'll buy you a J2O if you get down in one piece!" he called out.

The ridiculousness of that remark made her smile and brought her senses back into focus. She managed to say, "... and a packet of crisps?"

Quicksilver clung tightly to the sides of the ladder, Giorgio below her, minding that each of her steps was planted firmly on a metal rung.

Thirty second later and both were standing on the

floor of the circus ring. They hugged each other.

"You saved my life!" Quicksilver said.

"Maybe," Giorgio replied. "Now we need to find out who tried to take it away!"

*

The ringmaster spread his arms to the spectators. "You have just witnessed another extraordinary act of courage by our intrepid performers. A round of applause, please, for Giorgio and Quicksilver!"

The audience clapped and cheered

enthusiastically and the pair raised their arms in acknowledgement.

As they escaped through the curtain, Quicksilver grinned at Giorgio.

"May I have my J2O, please?"

"Of course. I always keep my promises. Just one more thing though ..."

Quicksilver frowned.

"You didn't say which flavour crisps you wanted."

* * *

After that evening's performance came to an end and the remaining spectators had finally departed, Josh Brown, the circus manager, walked across to Giorgio.

"I want you, Ian and Andy to come across to my caravan. I want to know what went wrong up there tonight."

* * *

"Somebody must have loosened the fixings after I'd fixed them in place," Giorgio said.

"Oh, Giorgio, why would you want to go and do

a thing like that?" Andy asked mockingly.

"Don't be a bigger idiot than you already are," Giorgio retorted.

Josh raised his hand. "I can do without you two bickering. Somebody might have been killed to tonight."

"I double-checked it like I usually do," Peter said. "It was fine, although…"

"Although what?" Josh asked.

"It's nothing really but after we'd set it up last night … before tidying up … I thought I saw someone at the top of the ladder but it was dark so I can't be sure."

Josh looked questioningly at Giorgio.

"Giorgio?"

"It wasn't me!" he said indignantly.

"Of course, you would say that," Andy responded with an evil grin.

"Okay. That's enough. Let's just be thankful nobody was hurt."

Giorgio scowled at Andy and walked away.

* * *

"I hope you will find this flavour satisfactorily," Giorgio said as he handed a bottle of J2O to Quicksilver.

"Orange and Passionfruit. My favourite!"

"Do you think …"

"Do I think what?" Quicksilver asked.

"Do you think I might call you something else?"

"So long as it's not something rude!"

"I doubt your parents named you Quicksilver."

Louisa chortled.

"No, of course not! I'm Louisa."

"Well, Louisa … I have something for you."

"What … *more* gifts?"

"Especially for you."

Giorgio grinned as he handed her a packet of cheese and onion crisps.

* * *

Charlie Cheerful, principal clown of *The Circus Maximus*, was feeling anything but cheerful. He thought he had been about to lose Quicksilver but she had descended safely from her swing. He supposed he should be grateful to Giorgio for his quick-thinking - and he was – but he longed to have been the one to climb the steps of that ladder and to help her down safely. His heart ached. His white face-paint might hide his tears but couldn't paint away the sadness in his heart or the tears in his eyes. Sometimes clowns even cry.

* * *

Andy Roberts and Ian Maddock had slipped out

between performances for a quick drink at a nearby pub. The routine checks for the evening's performance had been made and the time was their own for the next couple of hours. Giorgio had opted to stay in his caravan and catch up on some sleep.

"What do you reckon went wrong last night?" Ian asked.

"You mean with the beam?"

"Well, yeah. It was secure after we'd set it up. You double-checked it. I don't see how a bolt could have come loose."

"Well, if somebody slackened it off, and it wasn't one of us, that just leaves Giorgio."

"You reckon?" Ian said. "Why would he do that? I don't see him wanting to harm her. He's quite sweet on her."

"Poor little Quicksilver. What does she reckon happened?"

"I don't know. She doesn't have much to do with me. Have *you* spoken to her?"

"Nah. She seems to be avoiding me," Andy

replied. "Stuck up little bitch."

"Hey, come on! She's not like that. Not with me, anyway."

"I asked her out on a date after we'd shut down the Oxford do. She said she didn't mix business with pleasure."

"So what's with her and Giorgio then?"

Andy took a swig of his beer.

"Maybe he wants to apologise for almost killing her last night," Andy said.

"You think so?"

"Well, it wasn't me tampered with the beam. Was it *you*?"

"Don't be daft, mate. I wouldn't want to hurt her."

"Well, there you are then. That just leaves Giorgio, doesn't it?"

Ian shrugged his shoulders.

"I just don't see it."

* * *

Quicksilver stood trembling behind the curtain. The audience had begun clapping their appreciation of the clowns and it was only a matter of moments before the ringmaster would introduce her. She might have been crippled last night. She would rather die than that. She hesitated.

It suddenly became quiet on the other side of the curtain. The ringmaster would have raised and spread his arms. In a moment or two he would say,

"Ladies and Gentlemen, small children and big children, young or old ... welcome to The Circus Maximus. I hope you enjoyed watching our clowns. They will return later with another ten minutes of ridiculous and juvenile behaviour."

The circus light dimmed and a spotlight fell on the

ringmaster.

"It is now my pleasure ... nay, an honour ... to introduce to you someone whose performances have stunned and delighted audiences across Britain. With her trademark chiffon scarf and death-defying aerial display ... let me hear you welcome... the daredevil queen herself ... *Quicksilver!*"

The band struck up a fanfare as Quicksilver stepped forward into a beam of light.

She put on a bold front. A dazzling smile.

Shoulders back. A confident stride. She was expected to entertain a large crowd with a performance that involved very real danger. She suddenly felt very vulnerable but knew she had to confront her fear.

'I've done this a hundred times before', she told herself as she moved towards the ladder that would take her high above the heads of her excited

audience.

Quicksilver put her left foot on the first rung of the rope ladder, took three more steps and turned towards the sea of excited faces. She flourished her chiffon scarf, posed for several moments and then continued her ascent.

She began to relax a little. The ladder felt firm and stable. A dozen steps above her was the platform and swinging gently above it was the trapeze bar. This was the comfortable part. What lay ahead would become increasingly precarious and the danger multiplied a hundred-fold.

This was not a moment to feel timid. There *were* no timid high-wire performers. The price was too high. There would shortly come the point where she would leap from the small platform and grab hold of the bar with both hands to initiate her first swing. Timing and coordination, gaining the right speed and momentum ... *and then letting go!*

Quicksilver was aware of the silence that surrounded her and the sea of dimly-lit faces looking up at her from below. *Suppose she fell!* That was a risk she had faced numerous times. Them a thought lodged itself in her mind. Before last night, the beam supporting her display had never given cause for concern. Was last night's accident a woeful act of negligence on the part of the crew ... *or could it have been deliberate?*

Quicksilver pushed that thought to the back of her mind. She trusted them ... she had to ... there was no choice.

She took hold of the chiffon ribbons and launched herself into space.

*

"Thank you, Quicksilver," the ringmaster said.

"Let's applaud her bravery and her skill as an artiste of the highest order."

Quicksilver acknowledged the applause but it was only as she made her exit from the ring that the enormity of what she had just accomplished came home to her. She certainly felt she deserved the drink that Giorgio had offered to buy her that evening at an inn close to the circus.

Giorgio had said there was something fairly

important that he wanted to tell her.

* * *

"I'm intrigued to hear what it is you want to tell me," she said as they settled at a table in a corner of the saloon.

"The boss is calling in a guy to inspect the beam you were on the other night," Giorgio said. Louisa was startled. She hadn't been expecting this.

"A guy ..." she began. "He's calling in a guy? Why is he doing that? When?"

"First thing tomorrow morning before my team go

in to check things out. I heard him on the phone."

"How come? Where were you?"

"Outside his caravan door. I was about to knock but overheard him talking to someone and didn't want to interrupt."

"So you were eavesdropping?"

Giorgio looked puzzled. *"Ears dropping?"*

Louisa giggled.

"No, *eavesdropping*. I looked it up once. It's an old English word to describe the water that fell from the eaves of a house. Later, it came to mean the actual ground where that water fell."

"Your language ... English. It is very curious. I heard him say that he was worried about the structure of a beam that he thought might have become loose."

"Don't remind me!"

"He said it had never happened before and that his team were very experienced."

Louisa remained silent for a few seconds and then took Giorgio's hand in hers.

"You were a knight in shining armour. You probably saved my life."

Giorgio looked puzzled.

"What is a shining night? You mean like the moon and stars?"

Louisa laughed. "Not quite! I'll explain after we've finished our drink and on our way back to the circus."

* * *

William Northrop was proud of the circus he had founded. He was both owner and ringmaster. As a youngster, he had followed in his father's footsteps and worked his way up from selling candy floss to managing the ticket office. Now, many years later, he was talking to an independent investigator with many years of practical experience and a sound knowledge of circus equipment. Philip Hoskins had that knowledge. In his younger days he had been responsible for the aerial rigging of a travelling circus. He could strip down, examine and, if necessary, rebuild equipment.

"Louisa Turner, *Quicksilver*, an aerial performer almost came to grief the other night," William explained. "She felt the beam supporting her swing coming away from its support. I took a look myself later. The bolts had not been fully tightened."

"Have you spoken to the crew responsible for the apparatus?" Philip asked.

"Andy Matthews heads up that team. He said it was fine after he'd double-checked it but ... "

"But?"

"He says he thought he saw Giorgio up there in the rigging late that evening when I would have expected the tent should have been empty."

"Have you spoken to this man ... Giorgio?"

"I think Andy was mistaken. I have absolute trust in Giorgio."

"Okay. Well, I think I'd best take a look. I guess you have a performance this evening?"

"This afternoon, in fact," William replied.

"Okay. I'll check it out now. I'll begin by looking for anything obvious. I'll be as quick as I can ... always bearing in mind that if there is something amiss you may not be able to use it tonight."

William frowned.

"Better to scowl than murder most foul, eh?" Philip said noting William's expression.

William shrugged his shoulders. He thought of Quicksilver perched precariously on her high perch.

"Better the moans than broken bones, I suppose!"

Andy Roberts made a point of bumping into Louisa as she headed towards the mobile canteen for a midday snack.

"I was worried you were going to come a cropper last night," he said.

"The thought did go through my mind," Louisa replied. She shivered at the thought.

"What was it then? Something to do with the fixings?"

"That's the thing. Your team had checked it all out beforehand but nobody reported any sort of problem."

"There was nothing to report," Andy said. "It all looked fine when I looked things over. He frowned. "Although ..." He paused.

"Although what?"

"I thought I saw Giorgio slipping back into the tent after dark a night back. The night before last, in fact. Whoever it was had a torch and a hood over his head. Obviously didn't want to be seen or recognised."

"Giorgio? Can't be. Once I'd got changed I went down to the inn with him. After that ... well, I just needed someone to talk to."

"All night?"

"Well, no, of course not. We left the place about ten He would never do anything to hurt me."

"That sounds about right," Andy said. "What do you mean?"

"It was the night before that I thought I caught him sneaking into the tent."

"What? Impossible! He would have said."

"What? You think he would have said ...

'Quicksilver, I thought I should mention that I've tampered with your beam so you'd better watch out when you're up there. You don't want to hurt someone when you land in their lap, do you?'"

"That's ridiculous!" Louisa said indignantly.

"Think about it, that's all I'm saying."

* * *

Louisa *did* think about it. Thinking about it in bed kept her awake for some time. However much she considered Andy's words, she could find no pathway into believing that Giorgio would want to harm her. Quite the opposite, in fact. He seemed attracted to her. She wouldn't mind a date or two to discover more about him.

* * *

"It all looks fine up there," Phillip said after completing his inspection. "The maillons connecting the rope assemblies are in good order ... no damaged metal, no loose or broken links. The threaded sleeves should do the job for at least another year. We could take another look after that."

William looked thoughtful.

"Giorgio said he had to tighten the bolts when he went back to check why Quicksilver was left dangling precariously from her bar. He said the mountings had been slackened and when she applied pressure to them they worked themselves dangerously loose."

"Hmm. That's odd. If I was a forensics expert I suppose I'd be looking for fingerprints and checking them off against your maintenance crew."

"Heavens forbid!" William exclaimed. "Let's not go down that route."

* * *

Charlie Cheerful was in love with Quicksilver. It pained him to see her risking her life way up above the ring, twisting and turning, a nightly battle against gravity whilst below her a sea of faces were dazzled by her twists and turns.

Charlie had spent enough time in circuses to know that accidents through negligence were a rare event.

Over the years, there had been several high-profile circus accidents, including trapeze and high-wire falls and equipment malfunctions. They were rare but any activity involving acrobatics carries inherent risks despite rigorous training and strict safety protocols. An aerial performer must have faith in her belief that there will be something to grab hold of to support her and propel her forward.

* * *

After Philip had concluded his safety report he prepared to leave the circus grounds but was intercepted by Andy who asked, "Everything okay?"

"Oh, I think so," Philip replied. "He accepted my findings but I'm telling you – if you ever pull another stunt like that, I'm straight off to the nearest police station."

Andy smirked. "Fair enough."

"Now, before I drive off ... where's my money?" Philip wanted to know.

"Okay, okay." Andy reached into his jacket and withdrew an envelope. "I think you'll find it's all there."

* * *

When accidents to trapeze artists do happen in circuses and tend to me of a dramatic nature. Louisa had made a point of reading about them. Several had been due to technical issues and others by mistakes made by the performer.

Dessi Espana had been an aerial chiffon acrobat at Ringling Brothers and Barnum & Bailey circus.

In May 2004, she fell from a height of 10 meters due to technical failure. She died in hospital from the injuries.

Eva Garcia worked at Hippodrome Circus in Great Yarmouth, England, and was an aerial silks acrobat since she was 7. In August2003, she lost her grip and fell.

Sarah Guyard-Guillot was an acrobat at "Cirque de Soleil" and fell from a complex platform at and height of 30 meters during an act on June 29, 2013. She died on her way to the hospital.

The St Louis Trapeze Accident happened in 1872, when Fred Lazelle and Billy Millson fell to the ground when the trapeze construction failed. They fell on George North, a gymnast, underneath, and all three men were injured to the point where they didn't perform anymore.

The Flying Wallendas were a stunt performer family that, in 1962, had an accident on a tightrope. They performed their "Seven-Person Chair Pyramid" act when a leading man faltered.

Three men fell, two died, and one was left paralysed.

Two nights later, Giorgio and Louisa were enjoying another drink and a packet of cheese and onion crisps at the inn. There were four nights of performances remaining and it was good to sit amongst pub-goers who had no idea she was a circus performer.

"That inspector ... you trust him?" Louisa asked unexpectedly.

"What's brought this on all of a sudden?"

Giorgio asked. "It's something the rigger said to me earlier ..."

"He's part of your maintenance crew, right?"

"Yes, that's right. It's probably nothing but ..."

"But *what?*"

"He saw Andy pass something to that circus inspector ... he said it might have been an envelope."

"Containing a birthday card, perhaps? What's the problem?"

"I passed Andy on my way over to your caravan earlier and asked him whether he knew the inspector."

"I suppose he gave you a rude answer! You two don't get along so well, do you?"

"He's jealous."

"*Jealous*?

Jealous of what?"

"Me and you."

"What do you mean?"

"Are you blind? Sorry ... that's ill-mannered of me. What I mean is that he and I are both in love with you."

"*What? Did I just hear you right?* Say that again, please."

"I'm in love with you."

"I *did* hear you right! Well, let me tell *you* something."

"I know ... you want to get up and walk away from here. You want me not to talk to you again unless it's work-related. You want ..."

"*Hold up*, mister! You're stealing my lines. I wanted to say that I love you, too."

* * *

A tent staking-hammer is useful not only for pounding circus pegs into the ground. It can have other uses, too. Andy Roberts was particularly fond of the use he had in mind.

* * *

Louisa and Giorgio walked back towards the circus hand-in-hand. As they approached the big tent, Louisa squeezed Giorgia's hand and remarked,

"It all looks somehow different now."

"What does?"

Louisa swept her arm across the outline of the big top as it stood in semi-darkness beneath a star-lit night ... but then gripped Giorgia's hand very tightly.

Giorgio winced. "What is it?" he asked in alarm.

"I can't go inside that tent again!"

"What are you saying? Of course you can! It's

where you work. It's where your adoring fans and ... admirers ... gaze up from their seats to watch your stunning performance on the trapeze. What's all this about?"

"It's about something Ian Maddock told me when I was warming-up in the ring early this morning."

"Something he told you? Something he told you about *what*?"

Louisa hesitated.

"If I tell you, do you promise to keep it to yourself?"

It was Giorgio's turn to hesitate.

"Go on," he said. "Tell me."

"Promise?"

Giorgio shrugged his shoulders.

"I suppose."

"*Promise*!"

Giorgio agreed reluctantly. "Promise," he said.

"He told me that he had found Andy's bolt-spanner and peg-hammer resting on one of the beams my trapeze is attached to."

"Could he be sure it was Andy's? *I* am the one that

always checks those fixing, not Andy."

"He'd written his name on the hammer in red ink. *'ANDY - HANDS OFF'*"

"What are you saying? Are you suggesting that Andy adjusted the fixings? What was Ian doing up there, anyway?"

"He says he was worried over how your equipment could have failed as it did. I told him I went up later and checked it out but he insisted on taking a look for himself." Giorgio held Louisa's head in his hands.

"It's as well that he did."

"What will you do? Please don't cause trouble with Andy. There's probably an innocent reason for it being up there."

"There can be *no* innocent reason for Andy's bolt-spanner and peg-hammer to be up there."

"So it's safe for me to perform tonight?"

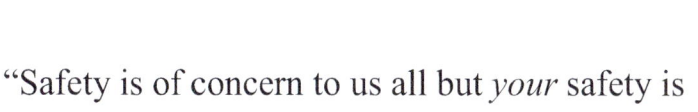

"Safety is of concern to us all but *your* safety is

more important to me than anything else."

"Okay, I'll do it. I shall leap courageously from my platform, chiffon draped around me, leaving behind the stability and security of your arms and taking a leap into space."

* * *

That evening, the circus was full. There was hardly a seat to be found as spectators packed the benches and children eagerly awaited the dimming of lights and the band to strike up. There was a buzz of excitement as the ringmaster appeared, looking resplendent in a top hat and tails.

"Ladies and Gentlemen, small children and big children, young or old ... welcome to The Circus Maximus."

He was greeted with enthusiastic applause as the band struck up a lively melody and the two performers dressed in the costumes of Roman gladiators strode towards the centre of the ring. They circled each holding a spear and trying to look fierce and intimidating as they stood either side of the ringmaster.

"Who is brave enough to fight me?" one of them called out.

"*Me!*" a youngster called out jumping about excitedly as his mother pulled him back down on to his seat.

"Anybody else?" the ringmaster asked but there were no takers. The two gladiators looked strong and menacing. That's what they were paid to do. It added to the wage they received for erecting the big top and maintaining and checking the equipment. Giorgio moved closer to Andy Roberts and withdrew a gladiatorial sword from its scabbard. He held it aloft. Andy did the same.

The two gladiators now faced each other as the

tempo of the band's music increased. And then ...
to the amusement of the audience ... the white-
faced figure of Charlie Cheerful wandered into the
ring wearing his baggy blue suit and looking bewildered. He went to the nearest gladiator and poked him.

Giorgio snarled at him and the clown let out a shriek and scuttled around the ring a couple of times before hiding behind Andy who turned and proceeded to pierce

Charlie Cheerful's balloons one by one. With another fearful shriek, the clown set off around the ring again, his bushy red ring of hair flowing behind. He tripped up on his oversized shoes, hurtled into Andy and scuttled from the ring.

The audience thought the clown's antics were hilarious and applauded as he fled from the gladiators and exited the ring through the rear curtain.

* * *

The wailing of sirens grew louder as the ambulance raced towards the circus. Inside the big tent there was pandemonium. Children were screaming. Parents held them close and covered their faces. Circus staff looked on in horror as first-aiders bent over Andy's motionless body. The gladiatorial sword had pierced his chest.

* * *

The police forced the lock on Charlie Cheerful's caravan door. There had been no response to their demands that he open it and when they entered he wasn't inside. His clown's clothing lay strewn on the floor and it didn't require a forensics expert to recognise blood stains spattered over it.

* * *

Andy was stretchered from the circus ring to the waiting ambulance.

"Ladies and gentlemen ... tonight's performance will continue," the ringmaster told his patrons. "Those of you who wish to leave will have their money refunded or offered tickets to another show."

A few spectators with children rose from their

seats and made towards the exit. The remainder watched Giorgio fetch the ladder for Louisa's aerial display. Moments later, she stepped through the curtains and entered the ring to a slow, solemn rhythm from the band. Her chiffon scarves floated around her body as she swirled them through the air and slowly made her way towards the lower rungs of the steps that would take her towards the very top of the big tent. The band played subdued music whilst the drummer punched loud single beats on his bass drum. Each of Louisa's steps was accompanied by a dramatic drumbeat.

As Giorgio followed her progress his thoughts returned to is discovery of the bolt-spanner and peg-hammer. Andy hadn't enquired after them but then how could he as it would only serve to incriminate him. Either that or he had yet to discover that they were missing from his kit. Perhaps it would be better to say nothing just now. It might be wiser to wait for an occasion that would have greater impact.

Louisa had reached the halfway point on her journey to the trapeze. She swivelled to face her audience and glided the chiffon scarf gracefully about her body ... and then took two more steps up the ladder. Suddenly, memories of what had happened so short a time ago flooded her head and for a moment she lost concentration. Her foot slipped. She screamed. In a moment of panic, she grabbed hold of a rung and took a deep breath before continuing her ascent.

* * *

William Northrop felt both helpless and anxious. Giorgio had paid him a visit after last night's performance and explained how Andy had bribed the safety inspector to issue a *'safe'* report. What was the connection between that and the stabbing of Andy by the clown? Would he be held responsible for Louisa's near-disaster on the trapeze? Should he inform the police about what Giorgio had told him.

If the vindictive episode made the news the consequences could destroy the excellent reputation of his circus. Was there a link between the stabbing, the clown's disappearance and Louisa's trapeze act?

Giorgio had shown him the club-hammer. It clearly belonged to Andy. The spanner, too. He thought of Quicksilver twisting her chiffon scarf way up towards the top of the tent. If it hadn't been for Giorgio's prompt action ... who knows?

William sighed. Surely events couldn't get any worse, could they?

He heard a car pull up followed by a knock on his caravan door.

* * *

When William opened his door he was confronted by two police officers.

"We're looking for a member of your circus, sir. A

clown by occupation. A would-be murderer by design."

"Andy Roberts ...?"

"He should be out of hospital in a day or two. The blade didn't penetrate greatly."

"They're little more than theatre props," William said. "How can I help you?"

"We'd like to speak to his friend - the other gladiator. Do you know where we might find him?"

"That'll be Giorgio Fabrini. He's probably

catching up on some sleep in his caravan."

* * *

Giorgio was about to fall asleep when the police officers rapped on his door.

Cursing silently to himself, he rolled off his bunk and opened it.

"Mister Fabrini? We'd like a quick word, if you wouldn't mind, sir."

"Of course. Come in. You won't find it very tidy ..." and he pointed to his gladiatorial costume and rigging equipment laid out on the floor.

"Not a problem, sir. We won't keep you very long." The second officer was staring at the pile of clothing.

"You know, if I ever leave the force I'd quite fancy..."

"Not now, constable, thank you. Are you aware of any reason why the ... er ... clown would wish to harm the ... er ... gladiator? I'm sorry, sir, but I have yet to learn their names outside of the circus."

"The gladiator, the man in hospital, is Andy Roberts. The clown is Charlie Cheerful."

"His real name, sir."

"That's the name he goes by. I've never heard him use any other."

"Really? Well, we'll leave that for the moment. The other gladiator would be … "

"Me. Giorgio. Giorgio Fabrini."

"How well do you know Mister Roberts?"

"Not well," Giorgio told the police officers. "But well enough, unfortunately," he added.

"Unfortunately? That's interesting. Why do you say that?"

"We both share an interest in Louisa, who works

the trapeze."

"Could you explain what you mean by an interest?"

"She is my girlfriend. I rather think that Andy wishes she was his."

"You two are rivals, then?"

"I don't see it that way."

"What *I* don't see is a reason for that clown to attack your friend, Andy," one of the officers said.

"As I said, he is not my friend."

"You don't get along then?"

"You could say that."

"I just did, sir. Just why is that, though? Why don't you two get along?"

"I think he's jealous."

"Of your friendship with ... er ... Louisa?"

"Exactly. You know ... maybe I shouldn't be saying this ... but I think he tampered with the beam supporting her trapeze."

The two policeman glanced at each other.

"Why do you say that?" one asked.

"Ian Maddock, he's the third member of our maintenance crew, found Andy's bolt-spanner and a peg-hammer that he'd accidentally left behind on one of the support beams."

"But how can you be sure that either of them were his?"

"I'll show you."

Andy got down on his knees, felt beneath his bunk and withdrew a hammer.

"He wrote his name on this one!"

* * *

Charlie Cheerful was not living up to his name. Originally from Glascow, Angus Campbell thought *'Charlie Cheerful'* a good name for a clown in his newly-adopted circus role and sounded ironically appropriate for a clown with a downcast appearance. He liked living away from Glascow and its gloom and counted himself fortunate to have found work in a circus that gave him the opportunity to visit many parts of Britain.

There was one thing missing from Charlie Cheerful's life and that was Quicksilver. Not only was she courageous, risking her life performing acrobatics above the heads of circus patrons, in his eyes she was also very beautiful. Charlie knew very well that both Giorgio and Andy were attracted to her, too, and to have her to himself he would need to deal with his rivals.

"Well," he thought, "I have made a start."

* * *

Andy was discharged after spending the best part of a week in hospital having his knife injuries patched up. He was advised to rest for a further week before returning to his employment at the circus. Ian Maddock collected him from the hospital and on the journey back told him about a visit from the police.

"Did anyone find my hammer, do you know?"

"I'm pretty certain they did. It wasn't there when I climbed up to check. It was dark. Nobody saw me."

"Damn! The police will be asking me questions next."

"They've already been on site asking us questions. I didn't tell them anything."

"My initials are on that hammer, you know."

"Yes, I realise that. To be truthful, I don't know how you're going to explain it away."

"Nor do I. I'm buggered."

* * *

Angus didn't know whether Andy was dead or alive. If he had killed him with the gladiator's sword he'd have to go into hiding someplace. He'd lose his clothing and possessions but could see no way to return to his caravan and enter it unseen. If he could get a message to Louise, would she go into hiding with him or would Ian Maddock, Giorgio Fabrini or the police warn her away.

He knew Louisa was secretly in love with him and was not interested in the attentions of either Giorgio or Andy. He could see it in her eyes. He could see it in the way that, high up on her trapeze, she would pull aside the chiffon and look down upon him and smile. She hid it well. He almost felt sorry for his rivals.

* * *

Just as Andy had predicted, the police arrived at his caravan and drove him away to be questioned.

"A hammer and spanner were found on the beam securing the trapeze used by Louisa Turner for her circus act. The hammer had your name on it and the words *'hands off'*. Can you explain that?"

Andy hesitated.

"I think Giorgio put them there. They went missing from my tool bag."

"Why would he do that? Why would he endanger the life of a person he was fond of?"

"He was jealous of me. Louisa might not have shown it but she was attracted to me although she was playing hard to get by pretending to Giorgio that she was interested in *him*."

"I see. You want us to believe that, do you?"

"It's the truth."

"Let's get this straight. You're claiming that Andy Roberts stole two of your tools and then climbed a ladder, tampered with some fixings and then left them on the beam before climbing back down again?"

"Yeah. That's about it."

"We've spoken to Mister Roberts. He denies all knowledge of how the tools got up there. We will need to take your fingerprints."

"My fingerprints? Why? They're bound to be on the tools."

"Well, we'll take those of Mister Roberts and the clown, too, and see what we come up with."

"Suppose they were wearing gloves?"

"Suppose you tell us what really happened."

* * *

The police could hardly issue a warning advising the public to steer clear of a man dressed as a clown and not approach him.

Angus Campbell, or Charlie Cheerful to his fans, wanted Louisa to know he was safe and well but the only way to do that would be to pay her a visit.

There was little danger of him being recognised by anyone outside of the circus but he couldn't hide from those within it. However, if he could reach William Northrop, the circus manager, without being seen by other staff, he could ask him to pass a message to Louisa. In return, he would not disclose something he had overheard while he was awaiting to enter the ring from behind the curtain. Andy had let slip that he'd offered Philip Hoskins a bribe to declare the rigging safe and so exonerate himself of responsibility for a near-disaster. It was very unfortunate that Giorgio had returned later and found Andy's tools resting on the beam.

Andy Roberts would need to be dealt with. He had to be eliminated. That way he could argue that Andy, in a fit of jealousy, had broken into his caravan, nicked the tools, then lodged them on the beam in order to incriminate him in the near-disaster. Andy Roberts was too close to the truth.

* * *

Philip Hoskins felt guilty. He felt acutely disappointed with himself. What had led him to accept the bribe from Andy? Where was his integrity? If it ever got out, his reputation would be in tatters, nobody would use his services and he might even find himself caught up in a criminal investigation. Andy Roberts posed a serious threat.

He had to be eliminated ... but what if Andy Roberts had passed on what he knew to the ringmaster, William Northrop? Philip felt physically sick.

* * *

Phillip Hoskins considered himself a man of integrity so why had he allowed avarice to get the better of him? He lived comfortably and had no need of the one hundred pounds that Andy Roberts had offered him. It was a moment of stupidly on his part. He had seen tools on the beam, one with '*Andy*' written on it, but the beam itself had been secure when he tested the fittings. Andy, he assumed, had forgotten to take them back down with him. His report to William Northrop had been correct. The beam, when he checked its fixings, *was* secure. Andy's fear of the tools being discovered had cost him a hundred pounds.

What would a man of integrity do next? The answer became obvious. He would tell William the truth and suffer the consequences, Next, he would contact the police and tell them what he had discovered. Had he perverted the course of justice by lying?

* * *

William Northrop listened without interruption to what Phillip was telling him.

"I thought better of you, Phillip," he said.

"*I* thought better of me. I don't expect you to ask for my assistances in future, of course."

William remained silent for several moments.

"Have you mentioned this to anyone else?"

"No. The only people who know about this are

Andy Roberts ... and now you."

"I need hardly say how stupid you were. We go back a long way. I still have trust in you so let's just forget it ever happened."

"Do you think I should tell the police?"

"No. There's nothing to be gained in doing that. Tell me, how much did Andy give you?"

"A hundred pounds."

"I suggest you donate it to the Circus Aids Benevolent Fund."

Phillip nodded his head. "Thank you," he said.

* * *

Andy Roberts realised that Charlie Cheerful posed a threat. The clown was aware of the bribe offered to the safety inspector. Charlie Cheerful had also attacked him with a gladiator sword in front of a packed audience. A man who could do that was capable of anything. He had to be silenced. It would serve a double purpose. The clown wouldn't be able to pass on information to the police and he would no longer be alive and remain a rival for Louisa's affection.

* * *

William Northrop and Andy Roberts stood face-to-face.

"You lied to me about tampering with the beam."

Andy said nothing.

"And you gave my safety advisor money to not disclose his findings."

"And your clown Cheerful Charlie tried to kill me. Maybe I should press charges."

"It was an accident."

"Is that what he told you?"

"No ... but I think it best that you accepted it as such. That way, I will take the matter of your tampering with Louisa's equipment no further."

Andy looked sullen. "Do I still have my job?"

"No, Andy, you do not. You're fired. Now get out of my caravan and out of my sight."

"You owe me some wages," Andy said.

"I'll leave your wage packet at the ticket cabin. You can collect it tomorrow."

Andy turned on his heel, left the caravan and attempted to slam the door shut behind him but it rebounded and struck the back of his head,

"Do take care! You don't want to hurt yourself," William Northrop shouted out.

* * *

Andy made his way around the back of the circus tent and stooped to pick up a length of rope that had been discarded on the grass. He grinned to himself. What a stroke of luck!

* * *

Charlie Cheerful was about to knock on the ringmaster's caravan door. The grass around him was soft and silenced Andy's footsteps and the rope that Andy pulled tight around his neck silenced his scream.

* * *

William Northrop was well aware of the showbiz maxim *'the show must go on'* but it presented him with a headache.

Charlie Cheerful was a huge draw and children, in particular, visited the circus to see him perform his clownish routines. The business with the police out of the way, things had settled back into a more settled routine before being thrown into confusion once again by the clown's strangulation at the hands of an unknown assailant. A replacement would be difficult to find, especially at short notice, so he had coaxed Ian Maddock, the third rigger, to double up on his work and fill the role temporarily. Fortunately, he was a similar height to Charlie Cheerful, although rather stouter, but the clown's clothing being ill-fitting anyway, he made a passable buffoon once makeup had been added. The circus had another week to run ... barring a further catastrophe.

* * *

There was a packed audience for that evening's show.

William Northrop kept to his usual routine although beneath his genial facade he struggled with his feelings and his smile was forced.

"Ladies and Gentlemen, small children and big children, young or old ... welcome to The Circus Maximus."

Once the preliminaries were complete, the band struck up in clamorous fashion and Giorgio and Andy, dressed as gladiators, brandished their swords and paced slowly towards Ian Maddox, appearing for his first time in the guise of *Cheerful Charlie*. At first, he found it difficult to feign fear but as Andy drew closer and the expression on his face turned hostile, he backed away without any play-acting.

Ian backed away as Andy approached. He continued to back-peddle as Andy's gladiatorial sword was raised and the blade reflected bright light from the spotlights into his eyes.

"Well, I've got rid of one of you," he whispered softly. Ian couldn't hear him above the noise from the wide semi-circle of spectators that were packed beyond the ring but he was mindful of Andy's malicious sneer.

"Run, clown!" Andy roared as he took a step closer ... and run he did!

Giorgio looked on anxiously as he watched Andy move aggressively after the clown. He held his gladiator sword aggressively, sweeping it from side to side, taking a sudden, rapid step forward and lunging towards Ian. Giorgio saw an expression of genuine terror written on Ian's face and stepped between the two. Andy gave a short laugh and directed his blade away from the clown and towards Giorgio. The swords were made of metal so that they clanged when the gladiators' swords met.

William Northrop grew tense as he watched events unfolding. The routine had grown too intense, beyond necessity. He raised his microphone.

"Thank you, gladiators!" he roared. *"And now I have the privilege and great honour to introduce the brave ... the courageous ... the fearless ... Quicksilver."*

Quicksilver stepped forward into the spotlight and raised an arm. The ringmaster continued with his customary introduction.

"What do you think?" he asked the audience. *"Should we let her risk her life on the trapeze?"*

Younger members of the audience roared *'yes'* as Quicksilver turned around and began her slow walk to the steps that rose from the sawdust ring to their topmost point at the highest reaches of the big top.

The band played subdued music whilst the

drummer punched loud single beats on his bass drum. Quicksilver raised her arm again and began her slow walk towards the metal steps that led to the platform. There were enthusiastic cries of '*yes*' from the youngsters. Their parents joined in their response.

Louisa turned her head slightly and caught sight of Giorgio blowing her a kiss. At that moment, she realised just how much she loved him.

* * *

"I do hope your girlfriend doesn't slip," Andy

sniggered. "I'd hate for you two to be parted."

"Why don't you just shut your mouth? You say such stupid things when it's open," Giorgio hissed.

"Such sweet words, Giorgio. Is that how you talk to your girlfriend?"

Giorgio reached for the hilt of his gladiator sword.

"Go on then," Andy taunted. "... if you're man enough."

"You're not worth wasting time on," Giorgio retorted and turned away.

"*Don't you turn your back on me!*"

Giorgio moved towards the steps where Louisa had already climbed the first few rungs of the ladder and now half-turned to gracefully extend an arm to her audience.

"Did you hear me?" Andy yelled but Giorgio was not listening. He stood at the base of the ladder as Louisa looked down and hesitated for a moment.

"Look out ..." she screamed as Andy approached Giorgio from behind with his gladiatorial sword raised.

Giorgio swivelled his head. With a look of astonishment that quickly turned to one of terror, he threw himself sideways and struck his head on the metal ladder. Louisa's scream could barely be heard above the screams from the audience as pandemonium erupted inside the canvas marquee ... and then William Northrop threw his microphone to the floor and landed a clenched fist to Andy's head.

Andy staggered back towards the ladder, reached out, grabbed hold of the nearest rung with one hand still holding the sword in the other ... and began to climb towards Louisa.

Louisa felt movement on the beam supporting the ladder and cautiously looked down. Now halfway up the ladder, she saw Andy clawing his way towards her. Swaying back, she could see William Northrop several rungs behind him. With nowhere to go, she continued to swing slowly back and forth. Looking down, she saw an arena filled with scenes of pandemonium as spectators stood, horrified expression on their faces, whilst some even climbed the barrier around the ring and ran towards the ladder.

A spotlight focussed on Andy as he climbed the final rung of the ladder and stood on the small platform at its top. The entire marquee was suddenly illuminated as all the main lights were switched on.

Fresh sounds reverberated around the tent as police and ambulance sirens wailed and a voice, sounding like an antique acoustic gramophone record-player, told people to leave their seats and make their way to the exit.

Andy pulled himself up on to the small platform and held the rails either side. There was nowhere for him to go now ... other than down. Louisa was beyond his reach and William Northrop was one or two steps behind him.

* * *

Giorgio rubbed his throbbing head but almost immediately removed his hand. It felt so painful to touch. His memory kicked in and he swifty recalled Andy Roberts coming at him with a gladiator sword. *Louisa*! Was she all right? Andy's gladiator sword lay at the foot of the ladder that led to Louisa's trapeze platform. Shaking his head, Giorgio looked up and saw Louisa balancing on her swing. Behind her, Andy was tampering with the bolts that held the wires of the swing in place. Louisa swung away from him but as she swung back, Andy tried to grab hold of her. His hand clamped on to one foot but she kicked it away with the other. The momentum carried her forward again but as she swung back she tossed the chiffon scarf over her shoulder and into Andy's face.

Instinctively, he raised his hands. He screamed as the scarf wrapped itself around his head and covered his eyes. He stumbled backwards, lost his balance and plunged towards the circus floor.

William Northrop was powerless to stop his descent and could only watch in horror as Andy swept past him. Louisa felt lightheaded. She stood frozen to her perch, dazed, afraid to move and clutching the ropes either side of her tightly ... and then through the mist she heard Luigi's voice.

"Can you swing towards me?" she heard him ask.

"I'm going to fall!" she screamed.

"No you're not. I'm going to lower the swing. Just hold on tight."

"*I think I'm going to fall!*" she said once more.

"Please, Louisa, take some deep breaths. They've rolled out a soft-landing pad ... just in case ... but we both know you can do this ... and there's a J2O and a packet of crisps waiting for you when come down. Now, can you move slowly towards the platform?"

Louisa began to gently swing her perch and each movement drew her inches closer to the podium. One final step ... and then her feet were on firm ground albeit ten metres above the circus floor.

Waiting several steps below was Giorgio wearing a broad grin on his face.

"Don't step on my fingers coming back down the ladder!" he called out to her.

"Only if you agree to marry me."

Giorgio strengthened his grasp of the ladder as he disentangled her words. After several long moments he replied.

"Only if you agree to take up another occupation," he said.

"I already have plans for that," Louisa shouted down to him. "Now, *please*, would you move your hands before I step on them?"

* * *

Not all of the spectators had left the circus tent. A number lingered, anxious to watch Quicksilver step safely from her ladder. When she finally stepped off the final rung, she flung her arms around Giorgio and help him tightly.

"You're safe now," he said.

"I'll always feel safe in your arms," she said. "One thing, though ..."

Giorgio looked anxious. "What *thing?*"

"Where are my J2O and crisps?"

* * *

As they walked away from the circus tent, Giorgio and Louisa heard heavy breathing from behind them and turned apprehensively.

With a sigh of relief, Giorgio said, "It's William."
The circus manager gasped for breath.

"I'm glad I've caught you," he panted. "I just wanted approached the couple and to say how proud I am of the pair of you. I'm going to miss you."

Giorgio glanced at Louise as much to say, *'how does he know we plan to leave the circus?'* but it was William that came up with a surprising announcement of his own.

"I'm planning on retiring from circus life," he revealed. "I'm too old and too tired for all these shenanigans. At the end of the season I plan on moving to Cornwall to enjoy a retirement along the coast somewhere."

"I wish you well," Giorgio said.

"Do you have plans?" William asked.

Giorgio and Louisa looked at each other for a few moments and then burst out laughing.

"We're getting engaged!" Louisa exclaimed.

"And the circus?"

"Well, I'm hoping to start up a gymnastics club and coach youngsters."

"And Giorgio? What do you plan to do?"

Giorgio rubbed his head and grunted.

"Something at ground level! I quite enjoy gardening and mending things so I'll probably set myself up as a handyman."

"Good idea. Oh, I meant to tell you ... I will be inviting all circus staff to attend Charlie Cheerful's funeral next Wednesday. It's up to you, of course, but it would please me if a goodly number paid their respects."

Louisa looked at Andy, who nodded. "For sure," he said. "Do we know what's happening about

Andy Roberts?"

"I couldn't say too much until now but the police have brought criminal charges against him and he's to stand trial for the murder of Angus Campbell."

Giorgio looked quizzically at the circus master.

"Ian's agreed to be the new Charlie Cheerful, then?"

"On condition that he can call himself that."

"Charlie Cheerful?"

"With one small difference out of respect for Angus."

"Oh, and what is that?" Louisa asked.

"He's to be known as Cheerful Charlie."

POSTSCRIPTS

The word Circus dates from Roman times when arenas such as the Circus Maximus staged chariot races, gladiatorial contests and mock battles.

Joshua Purdy Brown staged the first circus in a tent or big top in America in 1825.

The modern circus was invented in London by trick horse-rider Philip Astley, who opened his Amphitheatre of Equestrian Arts in London, in 1768.

Clowns are sometimes nicknamed Joeys after 19th century pantomime star Joseph Grimaldi.

Leotards are named after the first star of the flying trapeze, Jules Leotard.

The word jumbo, meaning large, entered the English language because of Jumbo, an 11-foot-tall elephant that the American showman P.T. Barnum bought from London Zoo.

The first elephant to appear in a British circus performed at Covent Garden in 1810.

The Greatest Show On Earth begins with the most enduring and endearing seven words in entertainment: "Ladies and Gentlemen, Children of All Ages…"

The traditional circus theme music is called Entrance of the Gladiators and was composed by Julius Fucik in 1897.

Chinese acrobats first appeared in European circuses in 1866.

A 'josser' is an outsider who joins the circus.

Enrico Rastelli (1896 – 1931) could juggle ten balls at once. He is considered the greatest juggler of all time.

According to circus superstition, it's unlucky to wear green in the ring.

The word clown is believed to come from the Icelandic word klunni, meaning a clumsy person.

Cirque du Soleil is a modern day theatrical entertainment

company that uses circus techniques from all around the world. Cirque du Soleil was one of the first circus based companies not to use performing animals.

In the words of one ringmaster ...

"I am one of 38 individuals in the history of Ringling Bros. and Barnum & Bailey privileged with uttering those famous seven words that have brought The Greatest Show On Earth to life for nearly 150 years. "I get goose bumps…the hairs on my neck stood straight up…every time I hear those words I become a kid again…" are common testimonials. For those seven words are not merely the start of a show, but the promise of something extraordinary be not deceived by his bombast or airs, although he is the Ringmaster, at heart he is a glorified fan, who is as amused, awestruck, and dazzled as you.

The Greatest Show On Earth begins with the most enduring and endearing seven words in entertainment: "*Ladies and Gentlemen, Children of All Ages…*"

AVAILABLE BOOKS (March 2025)
'Whiskers, Wings and Bushy Tails'
(Stories from The Undermead Woods)
~ book series for children ~
Large print and double-line spacing

The Inner Mystic Circle

The Race

Curly Cat

Dotty Dormouse

Blackberry Pie

George and the Magic Jigsaw Rain! Rain! Rain!

Where is Dotty Dormouse?

Tap! Tap! Tap!

SwaggerWagger

Three Wheels and a Bell

The Chase

Blackberry Bluff

Rebellion

Autumn

Quiz Night

Black as Night

Sheepish Singing Sisters

Ollie Owl's Experiment (Part Two)

Good Deeds and Evil Intentions

The New Age of Barter

The Mouse That Scored

Links of Gold

Buttercups and Daisies

The Tick-Tock 'Tective Agency and the Case of The Missing Tiddles

The Mysterious Case of the Missing Scarecrow Carrots

Woof! Woof! (Percy Pigeon is behaving strangely ... once again ... and Ollie Owl is determined to use his wisdom and the academic books on the shelves of his library, to correct matters for the citizens (the whiskered, winged, and bushy-tailed of Undermead.)

BOOKS FOR YOUNG READERS ➡

Larger print and double-line spacing

Bollington – The Cheshire Cat that Lost Its Grin

Millie Manx (The Tale of a Tail)

Granddad Remembers (but is he telling the truth?)

Ninky and Nurdle (Stories from Noodle-Land)

The Playground of Dreams

What Can I Do When It's Raining Outside?

Buggy Babes

CRIME ➡

Time to Kill

Stage Fright

The Potato Eaters / Revolving Doors (Fiction based on fact)

Donald Dangle is on The Point of Murder

Black Pad

The Sad Story of Nicola Payne

Friday the Thirteenth

The Woman Across the Road

ROMANCE ➡

The Man from Blue Anchor

The Night of The Great Storm

TWIST IN THE TALE

Open Pandora's Box and what will you find? (**15 stories with 'a twist in the tale'**) ...

A Night at the Castle

Baby Jane

The Little Bedroom

Bulls Eye

A Problem at School

A Running Joke

The Cure

Old Rocker

The New Appointment

The Sunflower

The Christmas Fairy

Pressure

Promotion

Knock, Knock, Knock

The Letter

terry@terrybraverman.co.uk
www.noteablemusic.co.uk
Amazon/books/Terence Braverman/Kindle Store/Terence Braverman